because everyone
loves a good story...

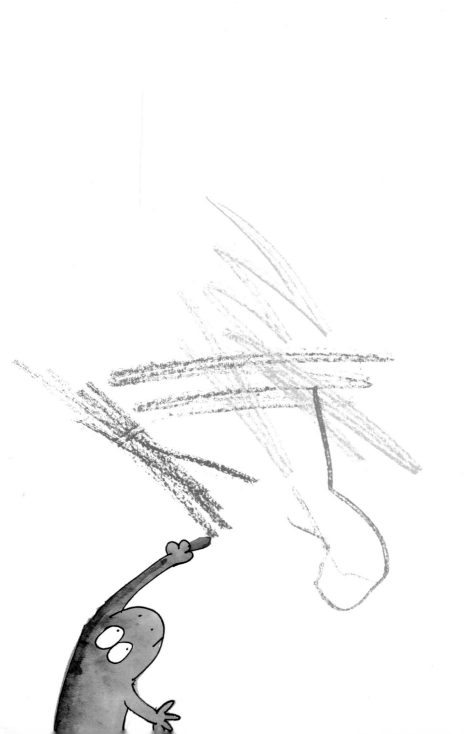

Jakob Martin Strid

Little Frog

ALANNA BOOKS

First published in the UK in 2009
by ALANNA BOOKS
46 Chalvey Road East SL1 2LR
www.alannabooks.com

ISBN: 978-0-9551-998-6-8

Published by agreement with
The Gyldendal Group Agency, Denmark.
Translated from the Danish *Lille Frø*, Gyldendal, 2005
© Jacob Martin Strid 2005
English text copyright © 2009 Alanna Books

One beautiful summer's night a meteor fell from the sky.

It went through the roof and landed
on the television owned by the Frog family.

The meteor cracked,
and inside was
a little frog.

Father Frog and
Mother Frog
hugged him.
"Oh how cute!"
they said,
"From now on,
you shall be
our little frog."
And they called him Little Frog.

The Frog family loved
Little Frog very much.
The two children,
Middle Frog and Big Frog
became Little Frog's brother and sister.

But, as time went on,
they realised that Little Frog was
VERY NAUGHTY!

One morning he got up especially early and drew all over Father Frog's face while he was sleeping.

Then he went into the kitchen and baked the telephone...

... and washed all the books with hot water and lots of bubbles.

Father and Mother Frog screamed:

"What are you DOING Little Frog?!"

Father and Mother Frog took Little Frog
to the school counsellor to try
to understand Little Frog's
naughty behaviour.

"I think you need to talk
to a specialist," said
the counsellor.
"Let me make an
appointment right now..."

He picked up the telephone
to make the call,
but **Little Frog**
cut the line!

Then he set the counsellor's
hair on fire...
"Oh, no!
Not in his bag!!!"
wailed
Mother Frog.

Father Frog was so furious all he could do was **SCREAM.** Mother Frog sobbed.

"We can't take any more of this behaviour!"

"Well, I've had enough" said Little Frog, "If you have to yell at me all the time, I'm leaving." And off he went...

...down to the railway station where he got on a train...

He sat down next to a lady with a spotty dress.

The train drove though the countryside...

...through strange cities...

...through cold and snow.

When the train came to the last stop, Little Frog walked on by himself.

Little Frog walked and walked.

He walked across deserts...

...until he
came to the
mountains...

...he walked right up the snowy peak until he came to the top.

At the very top there was a **cave**...

Inside the cave was a very **very** old man.
He had long white hair and a long white beard.
In front of the old man
was a very **old**, thick book.

Slowly, the old man opened his eyes.
"So, what can I do for you,
Little Frog?" he said.

"I'm
really
naughty,"
said
Little Frog.
"Nobody
likes me."

"Heh, heh, heh,"
laughed the old man.
"I'm sure you're not
that naughty.
You just need to
find a quiet
place inside yourself."

"Sit next to me
and close your eyes,"
said the old man.

Little Frog closed one
of his eyes...

...and then
the other...

...then he couldn't see anything...

Nothing happened...

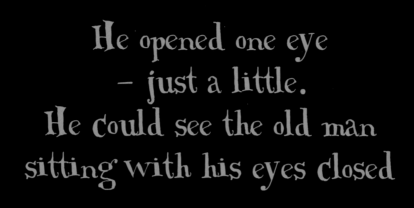

He opened one eye
– just a little.
He could see the old man
sitting with his eyes closed

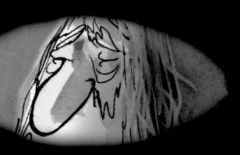

"This is boring,"
said Little Frog.

Luckily, Little Frog
had brought his
crayons.

First, Little Frog drew on the
old man's big, thick book.

When he ran out of pages
he drew on the
old man's face.

"What are you DOING??"
screamed the old man...

"You are the naughtiest naughtiest frog I have EVER heard of! Get off my mountain !!"

Little Frog rolled all the way down the mountain
and ended up in a heap of cold snow.

He sat there for a while, wondering what to do.
"I'm so naughty, nobody likes me," he said
to himself, "I have nowhere to go..."

But then he heard
a sound...

A helicopter!!!
It was Father and Mother Frog,
Big Frog and Middle Frog!
"Little Frog!" they all cried,
"We've been searching everywhere for you."

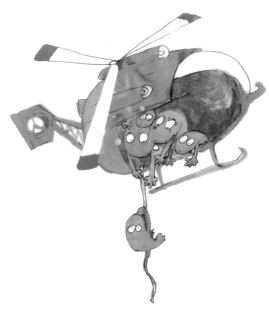

They pulled
Little Frog
into the helicopter.

"Oh, Little Frog,
I'm so happy we
found you," sobbed
Mother Frog.

"But I'm still very naughty," said Little Frog.

"You may be naughty," said Mother Frog.
"But, you are still
our Little Frog
and we love you."

Epilogue:

So Little Frog lived happily ever after with the Frog family. He was still naughty sometimes and they still loved him. He later became a big success and they put on a huge exhibition of all his naughty things.

More great stories from ALANNA BOOKS:
www.alannabooks.com

Lulu loves the Library
Paperback with multi-language CD
ISBN: 978-0-9551-998-2-0

Lulu loves Stories
Hardcover ISBN: 978-0-9551-998-5-1

In the 'My Friend' Series:
My Friend Jamal
Hardcover ISBN: 978-0-9551-998-1-3

My Friend Amy
Hardcover ISBN: 978-0-9551-998-3-7